USING THIS BOOK

*Children learn to read by **reading**, but they need help to begin with.*

When you have read the story on the left-hand pages aloud to the child, go back to the beginning of the book and look at the pictures together.

Encourage children to read the sentences under the pictures. If they don't know a word, give them a chance to 'guess' what it is from the illustrations, before telling them.

There are more suggestions for helping children to learn to read in the *Parent/Teacher* booklet.

British Library Cataloguing in Publication Data

McCullagh, Sheila K.
    Tessa in Puddle Lane. —(Puddle Lane. Series no. 855. Stage 2; v. 2)
    1. Readers—1950-
    I. Title   II. Morris, Tony, *1938 Aug. 2-*
    III. Series
    428.6   PE1119
    ISBN 0-7214-0925-3

First edition

Tessa
in Puddle Lane

written by SHEILA McCULLAGH
illustrated by TONY MORRIS

This book belongs to:

Ladybird Books Loughborough

One day, Tessa was out in the garden,
playing by herself.
Pegs had gone out
to look for food.
Tim was asleep.
Tessa chased a leaf
that was blowing in the wind.
The leaf blew through the gates,
into Puddle Lane.
Tessa stood at the gates,
and looked down the lane.

Tessa was out in the garden.
She looked into Puddle Lane.

She could see people in the lane,
but they didn't look dangerous.
"I'll go out into the lane.
I'll find out who lives there,"
Tessa said to herself.
"It looks very interesting."
So she went under the gate,
and out into Puddle Lane.

Tessa went under the gate,
and out into Puddle Lane.

The first person she saw close-to,
was Mr Gotobed.
It was a fine day, and the sun
was shining down on Puddle Lane.
Mr Gotobed had carried a chair
out into the sunshine.
He was sitting on the chair in the lane,
and he was fast asleep.

Tessa saw Mr Gotobed.
He was fast asleep in his chair.

Tessa went past Mr Gotobed very quietly,
so that she wouldn't wake him up.
She went on down the lane.
She saw Mr Puffle, at the door
of his house.
Mr Puffle was carrying a ladder.
He set the ladder down in the lane.
Then he picked up a brush, and
a tin of green paint,
and climbed up the ladder.

Tessa saw Mr Puffle.
Mr Puffle was at the door
of his house.

Tessa watched Mr Puffle
for a few minutes.
Mr Puffle opened the tin of green paint,
and began to paint the window
over the door of his house.
Tessa went on, down the lane.

Tessa went on, down the lane.

She was half way down the lane,
when she saw Mrs Pitter-Patter.
Mrs Pitter-Patter was out
in the lane.
She had no one to talk to,
so she was talking to herself.
She was cleaning her windows, and
talking hard as she worked.

Tessa saw Mrs Pitter-Patter.
Mrs Pitter-Patter was out
in the lane.

Tessa stopped to look
at Mrs Pitter-Patter,
but Mrs Pitter-Patter
took no notice of her,
so Tessa went on, down the lane.
She came to the end of the lane,
and looked out into the street.

Tessa went on, down the lane.
She came to the end of the lane.

A big dog was coming down the street.
Tessa didn't know it, but the dog
lived in the house at the end
of Puddle Lane.
Tessa saw the dog.
The dog saw Tessa.
The dog gave a great "Wuff!"
and began to run.
He was running straight towards her.

Tessa saw the dog.
The dog saw Tessa.

Tessa had never seen a dog before,
but she was **very** frightened.
She fled.
Tessa ran back up Puddle Lane
as fast as she could run.

Tessa ran back up
Puddle Lane,
as fast as she could run.

Tessa could run fast,
but the big dog could run faster.
As she came to Mrs Pitter-Patter's house,
the dog was close behind her.
At that moment, Mrs Pitter-Patter
stepped back into the lane,
to admire her clean windows.
Tessa ran round Mrs Pitter-Patter,
but the dog was running too fast.

Tessa could run fast,
but the dog could run faster.
She came to
Mrs Pitter-Patter's house.
Mrs Pitter-Patter
stepped back into the lane.

He bumped into Mrs Pitter-Patter,
and he sent her flying.
Mrs Pitter-Patter's legs flew up
in the air, and
she sat down hard on the dog.
"Wuff!" said the dog,
as she knocked all the breath
out of him.

Mrs Pitter-Patter
sat down on the dog.

Tessa didn't stop
to see what was happening.
She fled up the lane
as fast as she could.
The dog picked himself up.
He got his breath back,
and ran after Tessa.
Tessa ran on.
She came to Mr Puffle's house.
Mr Puffle was standing on the ladder.
He was still painting the window.
Tessa skidded under the ladder,
and ran on up the lane.
But the dog was too big
to go under the ladder.
He tried to – but when he did,
he took the ladder with him.

Tessa came to
Mr Puffle's house.
Mr Puffle was on a ladder.
Tessa ran under the ladder.

The ladder fell over.
The tin of paint fell off.
Poor Mr Puffle
fell down with a crash!
The green paint fell all over the dog.
Tessa heard the crash.
She looked back.
The dog was green!

The ladder fell over.
Mr Puffle fell down.
Tessa looked back.
The dog was green!

Tessa didn't wait.
She ran up the lane
as fast as she could.
The dog picked himself up.
He shook himself hard.
He shook green paint all over
poor Mr Puffle.
Then he saw Tessa,
and he ran off after her
as fast as he could.

Tessa ran up the lane
as fast as she could.

Tessa came to Mr Gotobed's house.
She was very near to the garden,
but the dog was close behind her.
She hadn't time to get under the gate.
Mr Gotobed was still sitting
in his chair.
He was fast asleep.

Tessa came to
Mr Gotobed's house.
Mr Gotobed was sitting
in his chair.
He was fast asleep.

Tessa took a flying leap
through the air.
She jumped right on to Mr Gotobed.
Mr Gotobed woke up with a shout.

Tessa jumped
on to Mr Gotobed.
Mr Gotobed woke up.

The dog was running so fast
that he couldn't stop.
He crashed into Mr Gotobed's chair.
The chair fell over,
and Mr Gotobed fell over, too.
Tessa didn't stop to see
what happened next.
She ran under the gate,
and into the garden.

The chair fell over,
and Mr Gotobed fell over, too.
Tessa ran under the gate,
and into the garden.

Tessa hid behind the wall,
and peeped back through the gate.
She could see Mr Gotobed
and the dog.
Mr Gotobed was on his feet.
He had picked up his stick,
and he was shaking it at the dog.
As Tessa watched, the dog turned tail,
and went back down the lane.

Tessa could see Mr Gotobed
and the dog.
The dog went back
down the lane.

As she was going
into the hole under the steps,
Tessa saw Pegs.

"Where **have** you been, Tessa?"
asked Pegs.

"I've been out in the lane,"
said Tessa. "I met a big monster,
and the monster chased me.
I don't think I'll go
in the lane again."

"That's not a monster,
that's a dog," said Pegs.

"And you needn't run away.
Just arch your back,
and spit at him."

"I'll go with **you**, next time,"
said Tessa.

Tessa saw Pegs.

I Spy is a useful reading game.
Use this picture to play it.

"I spy with my little eye something
beginning with..."

*(Give the **sound** of the first letter of the*
word to be guessed, not the name.)

*This is one of several stories at **Stage 2** in the Reading Programme. All the books at each Stage are separate stories and are written at the same reading level. It is important for children to read as many books as possible at each Stage before going on to the next Stage.*

Stage 2

1 **When the magic stopped** is another story about Tessa.

Tessa

There are two more stories about vanishing monsters:

3 **The little monster**

5 **The Gruffle** (The Griffle was friendly but the Gruffle was very gruff and grumpy.)

the Griffle